CYRIL LOOSESTRIFE

A B&W THORNTON BOOK

Published in 2015 by B&W Thornton Publishing

23 Henley Street, Stratford-upon-Avon, Warwickshire, CV37 6QW, UK

www.bwthornton.co.uk

Printed by www.flaydemouse.com
Somerset

First edition in the UK in 2015 by B&W Thornton

ISBN 978-0-9928040-1-5

Printed in England

THE MERRY MICE
OF STRATFORD

The Further Adventures of Stratford's Theatrical Mouse or A Fat Mouse in Love

BARRY THORNTON

Illustrations by Debby Faulkner-Stevens

B&W THORNTON Publishing

Barry Thornton

CHAPTER I

Pirates Raid Lucy's Mill

In the black of midnight, huge conker leaf boats raid Lucy's Mill. Coming quietly upstream, they slip into the riverbank; only a small jar of glow worms providing enough light to steer by. Teams of pirate mice sneak under the mill to the grain store, gather baskets of corn and pour them into the holds of their ships, then away down river to the food lockers, in Mousefield, Black Jack's citadel.

We have fashioned a beautiful house near the river, with a clear view across the open meadows, close to the site where our new theatre is being built. The house has one entrance door leading from the bank and four carefully excavated rooms, also a back door hidden beneath the bole of a willow tree. One room is to be a nursery, we have lined this with dry moss and sheep's wool and very soon we hope it will be in use.

Building Stratford's first theatre looked like a massive undertaking, but we discovered a willow with a gap between its roots, rather like a cave and there we dug beneath the tree, making an amphitheatre with a semi-circle of stepped seats. Assisted by at least twelve, willing, would-be actors, I managed to carry a triangular piece of stained glass, which was lying in an overgrown corner of the

graveyard and fitted it in position, so it covered the hole above the theatre. This should provide some light for the stage and some shelter if it rains. Two weeks later the theatre was ready for the first performance.

I, Kit the actor mouse, needed a play even the youngest of my brother mice would understand. Rumour had it that an old water vole called Cynthia Sneezewort had written a new play. She lived in a hole under the Clopton Bridge and was regarded by many, as 'quite mad', but she wrote poems very 'tragic and sad'. She had announced her latest venture would be a play about being miscalled a rat; a personal story close to her heart. Her secret love, a water vole called Cyril Loosestrife, had seen the leaf posters advertising her latest literary masterpiece and being very short-sighted he had mistaken Cynthia for a rat. Cyril had overheard mice gossiping about the 'mad rat' who wrote poems and with his heart broken he had fled to Warwick. This work would be the perfect play to launch the new theatre.

The actors read their parts and it only took a couple of rehearsals to make it all work, but as they began to read their lines it became increasingly impossible to stop them corpsing. It was not long before all of the actors were desperately trying to control their features and by the end of the first act, they were rolling around, helpless on the stage. I spoke seriously to them about the disciplines of acting. 'If you want to become great actors you must learn to control your emotions, channel your inner vole!'

When opening night came there was great excitement in the mouse community, this would be the first mouse theatre. The queue disappeared into the distance and every mouse carried a grain of wheat in their paws, which was the agreed entrance fee.

As soon as the auditorium was full, the play commenced, there was a special guest seated in the front row; Cynthia Sneezewort, the vole begetter of the play. Things went well for a while, then at a particularly sad moment, a reaction began in the audience, instead of the anticipated sigh, a quiet chuckle rose in volume, spreading from one mouse to the next, until there was a roar from the seats and many clutched their sides with uncontrollable laughter. The cast could stand it no longer and both audience and actors rolled around the floor, several had to be stretchered out. Cynthia was very upset, but also pleased by the pleasure the mice took from her play.

So great was the uproar that the play had to be cancelled; so ended the glorious opening performance of the new theatre. We attempted to console Cynthia, who was clearly devastated and when Robin appeared, from behind the scenery, he felt so sorry for the hapless vole that he instantly proposed a plan of action. 'I've been chatting to the bats down by the church, perhaps they can help.'

6

Robin strode off down the river towards the Holy Trinity; once there, he squinted into the gathering gloom, occasionally beating off clouds of midges. A pipistrelle, a tiny bat with a beautiful face, saw him waiting on the riverbank and hung from a willow branch close by, where it arched out over the water.

'Hello, I'm Rupert, I'm a bat'

'Really?' Robin demurred.

'Oh yes,' he unfurled a wing as if in explanation. 'Do you need some help?'

Robin being Robin, insisted on joining Rupert on the branch; so he carefully balanced along until he reached the bat, then he bent down taking a firm grip, hanging by his front paws. Carefully, he hooked his feet over the branch and was suddenly eye to eye with a startled Rupert. Robin smiled confidently, then losing his grip plummeted headfirst into the river. Robin was not a great swimmer, so Rupert sprang into action. Diving down, he grasped the mouse's tail, towing him back to the bank, where he shook himself dry, while Rupert laughed until tears ran down his elegant nose.

They sat together on the bank and Robin revealed his problem, how Cyril Loosestrife the water vole had spurned Cynthia, because being short-sighted he had seen her picture on a leaf poster, which looked, to him, like a blurry portrait of a rat, thus confirming that Cynthia was no vole, but was in fact the 'mad rat' who wrote poetry. The shame was, he was beginning to have tender feelings towards her, so with great sadness he decided to make a new life in Warwick.

'What's to be done?' wondered Robin.

'Well you could go up river and find him, he is probably still building a house or drowning his sorrows in one of those nightclubs that infest the banks up there.'

'It's too far, it would take days to walk to Warwick,' said Robin.

'If you walk, many of us bats fly there every evening, apparently there are more flies in Warwick. I've made the trip myself in the past. As a matter of fact, I'm the agent for a large horseshoe bat, he sometimes carries things up river for mice, and I take the bookings.'

'Could he carry me?' asked Robin.

'I don't know', said Rupert, looking at the mouse with his head on one side. 'You're slim enough, but he might need to stop a few times, we fit him with a cradle which hangs under his belly like a swing.'

'What would it cost?'

'If you're returning the same day, around 200 flies each way, including cradle, helmet and B.A.T.'

In no time all the travel arrangements were made; two days hence, Baron the horseshoe bat would be waiting by the riverbank, equipped with a cradle, leather cap and high visibility ruff. Robin began collecting flies in an ingenious manner; he used a jar of glow worms with muslin stretched over the top and when passing flies were attracted by the light and settled on the cloth, he gathered them, ready for Baron.

CHAPTER II

Up the river

Baron was not a pretty bat and watching him devour flies was awful. When his meal was completed he indicated Robin should climb into a fragile-looking willow tray, which he did with some fear. A label declared 'Made with pride by wood mice'. It had grown quite dark, but there was a possibility of a moon later, helpful for navigation.

With a great effort the horseshoe bat lifted into the air, to applause led by Helen and several would-be actors, all shouting: 'Good luck, Robin.'

Everything went well until Baron spotted a cluster of flies, just above the surface of the water. This resulted in Robin being dunked into the river, only to rise again dripping and covered in pond weed. Great was his relief as he was gently lowered on to the riverbank in Warwick, below the towering walls of the castle. Baron entreated Robin to hurry, as the dawn was fast approaching and he needed to get back before the day began.

Robin moved away along the riverbank and to his surprise he found he was being followed by more and more mice. He stopped and asked a mouse if he knew a water vole, who had settled in the bank recently. All the mice answered as one.

'You mean Cyril.'

'Yes, I do.'

'He's a very sad vole, he is, there's something missing in his life,' said one of the Warwick mice, cryptically.

'That's what I want to talk to him about, where does he live?'

'We'll show you, bet he won't talk to you though.'

When they finally reached the place where the vole was building a new home, a scene of devastation greeted them, for his bad tempered mining had collapsed a long stretch of the riverbank. Now he was excavating a neat hole in more solid ground, with a large courtyard for sunbathing and a small garden.

Robin called very loudly into the burrow, for what seemed like a long time, eventually a pair of dust-coated whiskers emerged from the hole, followed by an irritated vole.

'Who wants me? All I ask is to be left alone'.

'I've come to tell you one thing, then I'll go. Cynthia is not a rat, she's a water vole, like you and what's more she has loved you for years. Since you left she has been heartbroken.'

'But everyone said she was a rat.'

'Just come up the river and see for yourself. Now I have to go, I have a bat to catch, but don't forget what I told you.'

Robin travelled back to Stratford, this time with no stops because there was already a light in the east, anticipating the birth of another day.

Robin landed successfully near the theatre, confident that he had set the wheels

in motion and hopeful for a happy resolution. Baron consumed his second jar of flies

and left for his roost.

It was a case of waiting to see if the plan would work. We welcomed him back,

Robin had done a brave and wonderful thing, as few, if any, mice had flown before.

The one exception was the legendary Icarus mouse, who had fallen from a great

height into the sea, he was dropped by a hungry hawk, temporarily blinded by the

sun, as he carried the mouse home for supper. He survived by floating to the shore,

clinging to a long strand of bladderwrack.

In the meantime we had a theatre to run and a new play to find. I thought

the actors might be experienced enough to tackle one of Will's plays, possibly 'A

Midsummer Night's Dream' which was one of my favourites. Obviously I knew the

play well and thought I might devise a shorter version.

The problems started when some of the male mice objected to playing the

female parts. They flung off their floral headdresses and spoke in deep voices, while

stamping about the stage. They declared a strike before the rehearsals even started.

I sat down and explained that unless they obeyed my requests there would be no

theatre at all. Gradually they saw sense, I agreed to recruit some actresses for future

productions. One of the actors called De Vere was a natural for Bottom. He was very

funny and did a strange movement, which he called lunar dancing, which created the

effect of gliding across the stage.

The rest of the rude mechanicals were both rude and mechanical, but maybe they would do. We thought Rupert would be perfect as Puck, as he could fly around the world in 40 minutes, well our world anyway. The fairies would need wings and moths on silken threads were suggested, but the idea was scrapped when we realised that bats eat moths. We were worried that Puck might swoop down and eat Peaseblossom mid-performance and this would not improve the reviews, though some mice might enjoy that sort of thing. Eventually, we decided that fitting the mice with paper wings was a far better option.

Considering this was our first real play, it went very well and our troupe of young actors were improving with every performance. I had reason to be pleased and the actors were getting more professional, though I, Kit, took the part of Oberon and Helen played Titania.

Much to our surprise a petition was delivered to the stage door which demanded a new play by the 'mad rat', as they loved her special comedies and they claimed that they would picket the theatre until their demands were met. I refused to be blackmailed, but during the second performance of 'A Midsummer Night's Dream' the noise outside was unbearable. They carried leaf placards with 'We Want the Mad Wrat,' misspelt on them. I went out and faced the ugly mob, they weren't particularly angry, just less than good looking. We promised to ask her if she would write a new play and they wandered off dragging their placards behind them, allowing the actors to continue Will's play, there's no pleasing some people.

In the blue sky above Stratford a dark and threatening cloud blew in from the direction of distant Bidford, for the pirate Black Jack was gathering his forces, intent on revenge. A cruel winter stalked the happy scenes of harvest home.

It began with heavy rain that fell for two uninterrupted weeks, flooding the meadows on the far side of the river, but leaving us and our neighbours dry, on the higher ground near the church. In our warm, dry, nest, much to my delight, Helen gave birth to five babies and most of our time was now devoted to their care, how soon they grew bigger. One of them would escape the nest, much to our amusement, and our neighbours kept having to return him to the doorstep. Everyone said he was just like me, an adventurer, he looked like me too, so he was named Kit junior.

We had two beautiful daughters, Sara and Ruth, both were intelligent and loved the bright lights and fancy costumes of the theatre. Helen had no doubt of their future profession. Two more boys made the five, Ralph and Mark. Ralph was a gifted poet and thinker, while Mark loved the countryside. Mark kept a small farm with ants and glow worms, and an odd snail that walked backwards and had to be fed five times a day. He trained the snail to rear up and clap his horns together.

One day, I had a visit from the Stratford mouse council, they had heard of an imminent danger from pirates and wanted my advice on protecting their families. Since my arrival, I had supervised the building of a network of tunnels linking the most important places in town. Bakeries, food stores and Inns were all connected and guards were posted at the surface entrances, it was a rich source of food for us mice.

'We must make lockable doors for each entry to the tunnels.'

Wood mice were called in because of their special skills in carpentry and I decided to train a troop of mice as a military defence corps, 'my regulars'.

One morning, while I was walking along the river with Kit junior, we saw a young human seated on a tree stump, only when we got nearer did we realise that she was blind. Then, we really got a shock.

'I know you're there Kit, I sense your presence.'

She spoke in a perfect mouse dialect, turning her head in our direction.

'Don't be frightened I only want someone to talk to.'

'How did you know my name?'

'You probably don't realise how famous you are, I hear all the animals talking about you and your theatre.'

'Well I'm pleased to meet you, this is my son Kit junior.'

'I am delighted to meet you. My name is Eleanor.'

She stretched out her hand and we sat on her palm and talked for hours, it was the beginning of a long friendship.

'How did you learn to speak mouse?'

'It was something I discovered when I was very young and now I can understand most of the creatures around me. My blindness made me lonely, nobody had time for me, but I have the trust of all the animals and birds. Humans laugh at me, they think I'm talking to myself, but they don't realise there is a small animal nearby.'

When we had talked for a while, I told her of the new danger threatening Stratford's mice, for raiding pirates would mean a massive battle.

'We have no argument with the mice from Bidford, they are being forced to fight by Black Jack. If we could capture his henchman and ship them off down-river, all the other mice along the River Avon would live peaceably, free from the burden of these criminals.'

She thought for a while. 'Most of the animals I talk to would be willing to help, even my three cats.' Eleanor must have felt the shiver through her hand.

'Don't worry they won't harm you, although I can't promise that they were always as enlightened, they will do as I wish.'

'How can that help us fight pirates?'

'Well, I thought they might frighten the Bidford mice away, deserting Black Jack and his officers, if as you say they only fight because the pirates threaten their families, they won't have much stomach for seeing off cats.'

Soon after our meeting with Eleanor, the river messengers brought news that an army of slave fighters had left Bidford and Black Jack would be in Stratford within two days.

We decided to choose where the battle, or hopefully the non-battle, would be fought and needed a location best suited to our plans. We decided to occupy a small mound overlooking a valley, where a tiny brook ran down to the river. I sent my trained 'regulars' into the valley and had them dig a very large pit of

some depth, just above the line of the stream. They worked like demons, while our troupe of actors gathered sticks and moss using them to cover the hole, making it impossible to see, even from close by.

A message held in a cleft stick, carried by an exhausted mouse told us that the enemy was close by and heading towards our position. My 'regulars' came up the hill and formed a line just below us, with their pyracantha thorn swords facing where the enemy would cross the brook.

Eleanor approached the rear of the mound, where she could not be seen, she had three vicious looking cats on leads. To our amazement, astride the neck of the largest and gingerest cat, sat Robin, neither mouse nor cat looked comfortable with the arrangement, but both trusted Eleanor. Robin waved a sword and wore the curious aviator's helmet, he had adopted since his flight to Warwick.

When the enemy reached the stream, they began to cross, leaping from stone to stone, their tails dragging in the water behind them. My own troops were unaware of Eleanor and her cats, until one of them looked over his shoulder, just then the head of a ferociously spitting cat appeared above the mound behind him. He immediately took flight, charging down the hill towards the enemy. The rest of the 'regulars' thought this was such a brave and fearless act of courage that they all followed, bowling down the hill at full speed towards their foe. So great was their excitement that not one of them remembered the trench they had dug. They disappeared from view closely followed by the first ranks of the Bidford mice,

who were racing towards the 'regulars' to engage them in battle. The pit was too deep to climb out of without a ladder and the opposing forces made no attempt to fight each other, but sat about gossiping and eating their packed lunches, totally forgetting they were meant to be enemies.

Helen guided Eleanor, who had the cats by their leads and at that moment over the hill they came, with Robin, sword in hand, trying desperately to hang on to the neck of a rearing ginger tomcat. A second wave of attackers was beginning to climb the hill, but seeing the cats they turned on their long tails and fled for their lives, some were never seen again. This left Black Jack and his pirate officers stranded with no troops at their command, just at the foot of the mound.

'We must capture them,' Robin shouted.

Robin broke free, racing the cat downhill to cut off their retreat. There was a terrified look on Black Jack's face and his two officers just hugged each other and wailed. It was all over very quickly after that, most of the mice surrendered saying they were pressed into service on pain of death, or to protect their families held hostage in Mousefield, the pirate capital.

Suddenly, singing broke out in the trench, it was a traditional mouse hymn, an old folk song, 'A Song to Oolaf God of Mice'

Sing to the mighty god of mice

He keeps us fed and watered

With lovely bread and cheese

Which we think is very nice

Not all mice are great poets

In Oolaf we trust and invest

At which, many a confused mouse peered inside his shirt to check they were

wearing a vest. Beyond this the mice sang on with great gusto, but as no one knew

more than the first lines, most of them made it up as they went along.

They hauled the Stratford 'regulars' out of the hole on ropes and the Bidford

mice were allowed to make their own way home; they shook paws and left, vowing

to never take up arms against the mice of Stratford, ever again.

Robin and three others were chosen to deliver Black Jack to Gloucester; he

was led away, his front paws secured by a big knot in his tail. From there he would

be escorted to Plymouth, to be put in the hold of Sir Frances Drake's warship,

bound on a Caribbean raid, where lodged in the cheese store, he would be guarded

by the ship's mice.

I travelled with the 'regulars' to Bidford where we entered the pirate

city. Our first act was to topple a statue of Black Jack that stood before the land

entrance, then we broke open the grain store and distributed corn to the starving

families nearby. Mice appeared from everywhere, so I left a trusted mouse to

ensure each mousehold received a fair share and to arrange elections for a Bidford

mouse council, to bring much needed justice. It was a pity they spent half the

stored grain on building a massive town hall, but I suppose that's the cost of democracy.

The first people to greet us on our return home, were Cynthia and Cyril, now a couple. All the work of Robin, who unfortunately was not there to congratulate them personally. They were both very happy now and Cynthia expressed a wish to write a play for the theatre. I told her, 'I know you're gloriously happy, but what I want you to write is a terribly sad work, in your old style, we have had a petition from a group of protesters demanding that very thing.'

'I'll certainly try.'

'Make it as volely as possible and twice as sad as you can imagine.'

'Congratulations on your victory, it'll make the riverbank a safer place, and not a single mouse injured, wonderful', enthused a cheerful Cyril, who clapped me on the back, so hard, it was all I could do to breathe.

I would have to thank Eleanor for her massive help during the conflict and I would, as soon as possible. I didn't however, relish thanking the cats in person, but I might shout my thanks from a discrete distance.

At last life could return to normal, or so we thought.

CHAPTER III

New Cats and How to Hire a Mole

Meanwhile, there were three new cats at Lucy's Mill and a meeting was called, attended by members of the mouse council. Robin and I were there, along with Kit Junior, who was beginning to take an interest in the town's problems. Lucy's Mill contained half our winter food, the other half came from the pubs and bakeries, through the tunnels we had constructed.

I spoke first, 'We must deal with the cat problem, we cannot lose our free food. I've spoken to Eleanor and she says she will try to help.'

The other mice were pleased with this, even though we had no guarantee of success. I was sure she would come up with something.

Eleanor began to feed the cats at the Mill, gradually luring them further and further away from the buildings and she had a secret weapon. She had a wide knowledge of herbs and wild flowers and knew that cat nip sprinkled on their food would drive the animals wild. The three cats spent more and more time away from the Mill and we had time to hatch a plan, in their absence.

CHAPTER IV

Gathering Worms

We needed a mole to dig a much wider tunnel, so we mice could carry away large quantities of corn in less time. Several moles were busy churning up the pasture land opposite the church. Only one showed any desire to help us, but we would need to make a payment in worms, for this was the currency with which to tempt him. It required a hundred mice, who stood in a line and stamped the ground rhythmically, bringing the worms to the surface. Every worm was captured and a string tied round its middle, which was then attached to a peg. Our efforts were soon noticed by a raucous band of starlings who began to fly off with the fruits of our labours. After much stamping and even more chasing of birds, we obtained enough worms to satisfy the mole and after studying the soil structure, in great detail, he began to tunnel.

After three days, a super highway had been constructed into the heart of the grain store and with great skill the mole fashioned the end of the tunnel so it could be disguised by a discarded fragment of a broken mill stone. With our supply of food secure, we could return to our everyday cares and ambitions.

CHAPTER V

The New Play

Cynthia delivered the new play, but when I asked her to tell me a little about the work, she merely stared silently into the middle distance, wiped a tear from her eye, turned on her heel and left. The manuscript took up 40 leaves and was truly awful, she had excelled herself. I couldn't wait to show it to the actors, we called a meeting of the most responsible of the mice, so I could gauge their reaction.

Rehearsal started with a scene in which a much-loved hero died, I warned them that they must be sad and not to roll around the floor as before. A body was placed on a bier with a thorn protruding from his chest. As the cast filed on stage, I watched them carefully, their faces showed nothing but a controlled anguish. A weeping lady bent over the body, in the saddest of poses, but her shoulders seemed to be quivering and at last she could control herself no longer and began a snorting laughing fit, it sounded like an angry piglet. From that point the whole cast were lost in waves of frantic laughter, even the corpse seemed to find his fate unbelievably comic and rolled from side to side clutching his stomach. I stopped the rehearsal and gradually the laughter subsided. The actors were sure they would be told off, but I merely thanked them and said I was very pleased, which puzzled them.

The first night opened with the dead hero being slowly carried across the stage, a young lady mouse was draped over the apparently lifeless body. The cause of death seemed to be a large pyracantha thorn protruding from his chest. The makeup department had covered his face in flour, so he did look a little deader than the average mouse. A group of friends mourned his passing. The lady mouse was grieving ferociously, interspersing deep sighs with loud wails. As she bent down close to the head of her beloved, she managed to blow on the face of the dead mouse, which unexpectedly sent flour up the deceased's nose. She had to hide a wide smile behind her paws, while the dead body tried not to sneeze, as you know stopping a sneeze is virtually impossible. His body began to convulse, until unable to suppress it any longer, he let out the loudest sneeze anyone had ever heard. The audience loved this unexpected turn of events and cheered to the rafters, whereupon the dead mouse got to his feet and took a bow. Thinking on her feet the chief mourner shouted: 'It's a miracle.' She took out the thorn from under his arm with a flourish.

It was then that I noticed a broad smile on Cynthia's face and Cyril began to applaud. As the scene grew rapidly more chaotic the crowd grew louder. There was even laughter and cheers when an elderly mouse fell down a flight of stairs while carrying a tray. She staggered to her feet and asked: 'Anyone for tea?' This brought the house down.

The finale was a flying mouse who came zooming out of the wings, he

missed a cushioned landing and crashed right through the set, only to reappear through a closed door, still with his rope attached. The mouse actor was so shaken by his flight that he undid the rope and wandered off into the audience, much to the delight of the cast and the crowd, who slapped his back as he passed. The play was such a success that the audience refused to leave and their sides ached so much that some needed medical attention. A glowing actor-manager returned home that evening, tired, but happy.

CHAPTER VI

A Tribute to a Mouse Poet

After we staged Cynthia's play, we heard tell of a mouse poet, he had been very successful up river and in all the cities along its length, Marlowe would be coming to Stratford, so we contacted his vole manager, who agreed the poet would appear at our theatre under the willow.

He wrote of trees and the beauty of nature, baring his soul about the loss of friends from his younger years. He was quite well-off, but never forgot where he came from and had a twinkle in his eye and a passion for life. Some of his poems made the considerable audience shed a heartfelt tear, on this wonder-filled evening, in our little theatre near the church in Stratford. He was a great success and he made a promise to return some day. It is rare to find such sensitivity in a mouse, but alas he was never to return.

CHAPTER VII

Kit Junior Seeks Adventure

As if life wasn't exciting enough, we found Kit junior was missing, he had packed some food and left in the night. I had thought this might happen, his grandfather would be proud of this vagabond spirit and in spite of Helen's tears I reassured her that our son would soon be home, with a wealth of tales.

It was a cold and frosty morning, the day Kit returned home, he was chilled and hungry after his long journey. Helen was relieved and I was glad to be right, for once. She prepared a vast meal of corn and cheese: Kit ate as if there were no tomorrow. After that, he drank deeply from the clear pool we had made in the riverbank and stumbled off to bed. Our drinking water had recently been adopted by pleasure-seeking frogs, who seemed to regard it as a swimming pool, made just for them. The noise they made diving in and out and their construction of an elaborate mudslide, not to mention their late night singing, began to spoil the peace of our comfortable home.

When Kit junior finally woke, the next day, we got a blow by blow account of his travels:

I walked for several days, dodging the cats of Mickleton village and finally I climbed the hill towards Chipping Campden. While passing a field I came across

a weird contraption, unknown to us mice of the riverbank. Four oxen and a man were dragging a strange device, this was turning over the turf of the field, so now the earth was on top of the grass, very strange.

When I continued on my way, I saw an animal with a hard shell, which he carried on his back, he was puffing and panting and moving quite slowly. When he saw me, he gasped, 'Climb on my back, I'll give you a lift, I'm very low-geared.'

Well I was so tired, I decided to take Hannibal up on his offer. I dragged myself onto the tortoise's back and we slowly began to climb. The gentle rocking motion was very soothing and I was soon fast asleep, only to be woken when Hannibal fell into a hole, sending me flying through the air. After falling several times, I finally decided to follow behind, while trying to shake some of the dust out my ears.

CHAPTER VIII

The Great Games of Campden As Recorded By Kit Junior

After a day of travelling, I arrived at a hill overlooking Chipping Campden, where there was a strange gathering of humans. There were tents in which men were punching each other every time a bell rang, while other tents had less fighting and more food and drink. At times men chased each other up and down the hill and a group of humans was gathered round two men with straw tied to their legs, who were trying to kick each other, after many a blow to the shins, one seemed to be regarded as a winner and he got a prize. Other men were throwing each other in the air and diving on top of each other. There were beer tents and food stalls, which pleased me as there were many tasty crumbs on the floor. I sat under a table, where I couldn't be seen and feasted. What sights, what smells, what excitement!

There were archers, frightening birds of prey with bells tied to their legs and even more frightening men with bells round their legs, who waved handkerchiefs frantically. It was a beautiful scene.

All of a sudden, one of the shepherd's dogs discovered me and I was chased across the field, pursued by a growing pack of hounds. I ran and ran, until I was tired out, only just making it to a ditch where I fell exhausted. The dogs had discovered my trail and were lifting their heads to bellow and I thought I was

done for and kept perfectly still. At that moment a chorus of angry human voices shouted down the barking and the dogs were called away. I panted for breath, only when a few minutes had passed, did I feel strong enough to escape the field by moving from ditch to ditch, until the music and shouting were nothing more than a distant murmur.

While descending the hill, I met Hannibal, who was also returning, downhill. After some conversation with him, I invited the tortoise home to meet you and mum, but Hannibal declined, as the distance was too great for him, though he thanked us for this kind offer and said he might take us up on the invitation, sometime in the future. I was missing Stratford, so I decided to return home, also, truth to tell, the dogs had frightened me, just a little. I have an idea I want to discuss, perhaps we could organise a riverside games for mice. I can just see mice with straw tied in bundles around their legs, kicking each other to win prizes. There could be boxing, races, wrestling and even swimming. Robin promised us mice, he would teach us all to swim, in the river.'

CHAPTER IX

Robin and the Fish Rescue

Bad weather came and with it heavy rain, it rained for weeks and the river began to swell and flood the meadows opposite the church. It didn't affect our family or the other town mice, as we had long abandoned the lower ground on the far side of the great river, after floods in previous years.

When the rain finally stopped and the river level began to drop, it left pools of water on the meadows, just across from the church. Many poor fish were trapped, unable to return to the river and some were gasping for breath, in water too shallow for them to survive.

Robin ran up to where we were standing, demanding the mice act to help the fish in their terrible situation. He had an idea and summoned the 'regulars' by ringing a small bell, stolen from a horse's harness, ordering them to gather Butterbur leaves and sail across the river in convoy, where they would assemble and go to the smallest of the pools first.

They brought honeysuckle ropes which they tied around the fish's fins and fifteen mice hauled each fish onto a leaf, at which point another gang took over the strenuous task of dragging the fish back to the river, using the leaves like sledges. Once at the riverside, they slid the fish back into the safety of the waters. Robin

was magnificent, he still proudly wore his flying helmet and directed operations from a precarious perch, atop a Bellarmine jar, washed up by the storm.

When all the small pools were finally emptied and reinforcements from all over the town had arrived, they began to tackle the larger ponds. It was there that they discovered a huge and vicious-looking pike. Many mice thought such an enemy of the smaller fish, armed with razor-like teeth and so very heavy, should be left to its own devices. Robin argued that all creatures should be treated equally, even the dangerous ones. Much thought was put into moving this massive beast, particularly as it had huge, sharp teeth. However, it proved to be quite weak and allowed the mice to tie up its jaw with reeds. Twenty-five mice pulled for all they were worth and Robin sang a sea shanty he had learned in his youth, which helped coordinate their efforts. After a great struggle, the mice managed to drag the massive pike onto the three largest leaves they could find. Then, the fish was pulled along, sliding through the muddy grass to the river, where the exhausted mice rolled it back into the water, with an almighty splash. By the end of the day, they had cleared most of the pools. I was impressed with Robin's work and decided to organise a riverside party, for all the mice who had lent their paws to the rescue mission.

The next day, as we sat by the river, a strange thing occurred; while all the mice were celebrating, a large ripple rose under the Clopton Bridge, which gradually revealed itself to be a water carnival. Fishes rose to the surface in V

formation, speeding down the river towards the church. The fish were led by the pike, which kept leaping out of the water, arcing through the air. Robin and I couldn't believe our eyes; what a thrilling tribute. The mice lined the riverbank and applauded as the carnival passed. The fish came to a halt beside my house, from where we were watching and Charles, for the mice discovered that the pike answered to that unusual appellation, shot a fountain of water from his mouth, as the other fish slapped their tails on the surface of the river. Then, the pike pushed itself into the shallows and raised his head above the surface. Robin bent down and patted the monster on its back, pretending to not notice the huge mouth full of teeth, which seemed to grin at him. Charles bowed his head as if to indicate Robin should climb on his back, a murmur of terror rose from the assembled mice. But, the intrepid Robin, climbed on the pike's back and they roared away, across the surface of the water, leading the triumphal parade up to the Clopton Bridge, followed by hundreds of fish, large and small, in chevron formation.

This was how the fish thanked the mice for their rescue and Robin was returned, a little damp, but unharmed, to the shallow water in front of my house. Apparently the whole scene was witnessed by an old eel catcher, though the only person who believed him was Eleanor. Everyone else mimed drinking gestures behind his back.

CHAPTER X

Robin and the Mousetrap

It was nice to have Kit junior back at home and our walks along the riverbank could continue. As we walked through the churchyard on our way to Lucy's Mill, we saw a large gathering of humans dressed in their best clothes. They stood by the church door and then a man and a woman holding hands appeared out of the porch and the crowd grew animated and threw petals at the couple. Kit junior thought this quite cruel, but they all appeared very happy in spite of their finery being smothered in flowers. We decided to ask Eleanor about this strange custom and when we next met, she explained it was a human wedding, in which a couple pledged themselves to each other, for the rest of their life, blessed by the human God, no mention of our mouse deity Oolaf.

At home, the conversation turned to Robin who was always busy with new inventions and good deeds and Helen worried that he might be lonely.

One day when Robin was running along the food tunnels beneath the town, he heard a pitiful cry for help. Nearby was a small opening that led to an Inn. The hole opened into a space beneath a heavy cupboard. He carefully leaned forwards, hoping to see into the room and he could now hear low gasps of pain. Then, he saw her, she was caught by her foot in a spring trap and he rushed over to her side. The

young lady mouse had her delicate ankle caught under a vicious metal spring. He

quietly reassured her that he would seek help, trying to avoid attracting the cats

that he sensed were close at hand.

He dashed down the tunnels to where he knew he would find me, so I could

help him in the rescue. I sent for the 'regulars' and collected poles to use as levers,

within minutes a small army of mice was speeding through the tunnels with Robin

in the lead. I arrived to find Robin calming the injured mouse and asking her name,

she was called Portia. She explained that she had never seen a trap before and in

her hunger had been overwhelmed by the rich aroma of cheese and then snap she

was caught. She thought her leg was broken, but Robin said they would have to

lever open the trap before they could examine it properly.

I ordered my 'regulars' to gently position the levers and on my command the

trap was forced open and the leg carefully lifted away from further danger. Portia

was overcome by pain and a makeshift stretcher was created from two of the levers

and a scrap of cloth that had fallen from the cupboard drawer. Robin and I carried

the stretcher, it was a long and careful journey. Helen had already been warned of

the accident and had sent for Eleanor, who was well known for her ability to set

bones.

Eleanor came as fast as she could manage and feeling the small leg with

a delicate touch, she confirmed the bone was broken. She asked for some split

wood, the same length as Portia's leg and then instructed Helen how to bind a

piece on either side of the limb, creating a splint, bound with soft reeds that would support the bones until they knitted. Portia was weak with pain, so Robin brought her willow leaves and made a tea that soon relieved her agony. She was put in the spare-room where she was cared for by Helen and worshipped by Robin.

Robin was working on a flying machine, inspired by his bat experience. He had noticed how the winged seeds of sycamores spun gently to the ground. His idea was to make a harness and attach these seeds all over his body, including his famous flying helmet. He kept his preparations secret and when his flying suit was ready, he climbed up a willow and stood on the highest branch. With blind confidence he leapt into the void and for a while, it looked like he would crash, but a sudden gust of wind carried him skimming across the river and deposited him in a large and liquid cow pat. He staggered out of the mess, covered from head to foot, thank goodness no one had seen his fall. However, our son Mark kept a small racing snail stable and was gathering fodder, just as the mouse fell to earth. Though Mark was amazed at the flight across the river, all the other mice sniggered as Robin passed and held their noses.

Robin sought out a shallow, concealed spot, where he could wash and then made the long walk up to the Clopton Bridge, then back down river to the church, where he was to visit Portia, who was recovering well and even managing to walk, with some help. Robin arrived somewhat dishevelled, a little damp and covered in Sycamore seeds and sometime after the return of Mark, who was able

to entertain the family with the full story, before Robin could invent an excuse for his appearance. Both Helen and Portia howled with laughter and Robin was happy enough just to see the patient smiling. The first sign of Portia's affectation for Robin was her insistence that he never wore that ridiculous flying helmet again. She had decided she would marry him, the ceremony would take place in the church porch, with the smaller mice throwing handfuls of corn, which was to become the wedding buffet later in the day.

It was a wonderful, crisp morning, not all of the trees had shed their leaves and even the sun chose to shine brightly, Portia wore a beautiful necklace of hawthorn berries and green fern. She still limped a little, but that was to be expected after such an ordeal. Just about everyone attended, even the frogs made an appearance, they hopped up and down in the churchyard. Mice from the Bidford and Stratford mouse councils came and of course the 'Regulars', who formed a guard of honour. Eleanor had brought her animal friends: the cats watched from a distance swishing their tails angrily. A pygmy shrew held the two rings balanced on his long nose, each was skilfully carved from hazelnuts by a local wood mouse, who would have worked for peanuts, but sadly they were still to be discovered. White doves who roost in the window tracery of the church, lined the pathway, though they seemed as interested in the prospect of free food as they were in celebrating the wedding festivities. A loud honking drew the eyes of the crowd upwards in time to witness a V formation of geese, headed by two magnificent

46

swans, who swooped low over the happy couple, bringing a cheer from the crowd.

A great feast was laid out in the church porch, which may, or may not have been intended for the harvest festival. Robin and Portia, paw in paw, returned to a new home next door to ours, on the riverbank. The church warden could never work out why the porch floor was covered in corn.

CHAPTER XI

The Riverside Games

Soon after the wedding, Robin had a new project in hand, with the help of Kit junior and Eleanor, they set about organising a riverside games, which would rival the Cotswold Olimpicks. There were several surprise entries, so the festivities had to be designed to suit all the different animals and birds. The frogs insisted on competing in the high-jump and the swimming. The moorhens, ducks and nearly all the geese fancied the paddle race and the swans wanted to be judges of the water based events. Even a rather large grass snake applied to compete, but was politely rebuffed, as he obviously had an eye on the frogs. The young mice would be weight-lifting, wrestling, boxing and crossing the river on conker leaf boats. Teams of coxless threes raced from the bridge down to the church and Robin promised a secret event of his own devising.

During a spell of bad weather a large door had washed down the flooded river and lodged in a gap in the bank. The mice securely fastened it, so there was no possibility of it drifting away on the current. This became a perfect dance floor, on which a mouse band played awful straw recorders, while a mole sang sad songs of the dark. Fifty young mice danced the night away, swaying to these exotic rhythms. The boys saw the dance as an opportunity to meet mice that had caught

their eye, the male mice stamped their feet and tried to be noticed, while the girls

danced around their floral headdresses, placed carefully on the floor, Occasionally

they were visited by pleasure-seeking frogs, whose wild gyrations rocked the stage

so violently that a sign had to be erected 'No frog hopping' and the disappointed

amphibians left to seek their pleasure elsewhere.

In the coxless threes, conker leaf boat race, one sank, sabotage was

suspected. The winning boat forged ahead of the remaining competitors in spite

of covering the entire distance backwards. The mice from the sunken boat were

rescued by Daubenton's bats, who had stayed up late, and dragged the mice by

their tails into shallow water, where they were rewarded with a round of applause,

though a gnat sandwich would have been nice.

The young mouse wrestling matches were judged by Kit junior, which

proved difficult as both combatants rapidly ran out of steam and lying on their

backs, panted heavily. The event was won by a mouse who was large for his age

and Helen presented him with a golden grain of wheat, which had been carved by

wood mice and was suspended by a thread round his neck.

The shin kicking, was a particularly popular event, just think how funny the

scene looked with several mice tying straw round their legs and the more cautious

even wound straw round their arms. One of the two contestants in the first bout was

particularly wary and had wrapped his tail and whether by luck or design, managed

to clout his rival with his heavily lagged appendage, knocking him spark out. Kit

junior, who was the referee, stopped the fight and after reviving the stunned mouse, carefully explained that using the tail was strictly forbidden and any further use would lead to disqualification. After that, the fight went smoothly and both seemed to enjoy kicking the other mouse's legs, until it was determined that the mouse with the tail protector had lost on points. After many fiercely fought bouts, only one mouse was left standing and he too was presented with the golden grain, while the band played the mouse anthem.

Everybody made their way to the river to see the paddle race, though all the mice said the geese would win. The course ran from the Clopton Bridge down the river to the church. Paddling was the only form of propulsion allowed, but a certain amount of cheating occurred even so. A small tufted duck dived under the water and clung to the foot of a moorhen, only emerging to make a dash for the finish line, but he surfaced next to the swan who was judging the event and he was unceremoniously plucked from the water by the tuft.

Overall it was a great success and Robin's secret event was still to come, which would be the grand finale. All of the spectators gathered round a tent near the church, they chanted Robin's name, but neither Helen nor Portia knew what he was going to do. After a short time, a trumpet sounded and two of the 'Regulars' pulled the curtains apart. The tent flap opened revealing Robin dressed in a bright red cape and a new leather cap. All this was exciting and a murmur rose from the crowd, but more astonishing were the walnut shells strapped to all four of his feet.

Everyone shouted and cheered as Robin cautiously climbed down the riverbank on all fours and proceeded to walk out onto the water. There was more applause from the onlookers, though Portia covered her eyes, but whether from fear or amusement it was impossible to say. He gradually walked out from the shallows into the river proper, where the fierce current began to sweep his feet further and further apart. By gradually turning his feet downstream, he eventually gained control, but his new found confidence was to be his downfall. He became more and more conscious of being watched and the crowd gasped as he wobbled uncontrollably. Just as he was about to fall in the water, Robin felt a powerful lift and he was born upwards by the largest pike anyone had ever seen, it was Charles, who had leapt to the rescue of the mouse, but the audience assumed that this was all part of the entertainment. Charles then treated the watching masses to a fine display of powerful swimming, carrying Robin up and down the river. Eventually he gently landed the mouse at his home, where Portia dashed to greet him, it was a wonderful way to end the games.

The old eel catcher was crossing the bridge and witnessed all these strange events, but never said a word about it to anyone.

CHAPTER XII

The Return of William Shakespeare

One day, Eleanor was sat on the riverbank, waiting for me to finish a rehearsal.

She heard the clip-clop of horses approaching, which ceased when quite close by, a

rattle of harness and stirrups meant the riders were dismounting.

'Excuse me, young lady, I'm sorry to disturb you,' the rider realised Eleanor

couldn't see him and sought to reassure her, 'my name is William Shakespeare and

this is my friend Burbage, perhaps you have heard of us, we once performed in

Stratford.'

'Yes', said Eleanor, 'You are here to visit your family in Henley Street.'

'That's true, but also to visit an old friend, Kit, a mouse who acted in our

plays here, I understand that you may know where we might find him. Is he still in

the area?'

'Yes, he's famous for his acts of bravery and of kindness, but most of all

for his mouse theatre. He is a good friend of mine. His theatre is under the third

willow from the church wall, in the Dell that leads down to the river. It has a

piece of stained glass over the entrance, if you part the grasses you will see them

rehearsing the latest tragedy by Cynthia Sneezewort, a water vole who lives under

the Clopton Bridge. Be careful not to frighten them, I'll come with you, they know

me and I sometimes sit listening to the play.'

'You can understand them?'

'Yes, all animals, I can talk to your horse, he is very tired and hungry.'

'Well, I suppose I had better feed him.' Shakespeare laughed.

They sat together on the riverbank and parting the grasses they could see a rehearsal of 'Moon over Warwick' the very latest miserable comedy by the 'mad rat' Cynthia Sneezewort. William was amazed.

'This is wonderful!'

Just at that moment a messenger mouse, who was a friend of Eleanor and so not surprised that two humans were watching the play, dashed between them, squeaked twice and disappeared into the theatre.

All at once, all was silent, we had paused to hear the news, imagine my surprise, and I raced out to greet my old friend William Shakespeare. He asked me about the play and Cynthia our playwright, Eleanor rapidly translating from mouse to human and back again.

'Well, if you can get a translation of the 'Moon over Warwick' I might put it on in London.'

I was thrilled, but there was more excitement awaiting the mice of Stratford. Shakespeare told Eleanor about an idea he was working on, a new play, that we could try out in our mouse theatre, a world premiere. In our version it would feature a fat mouse in love and be called 'The Merry Mice of Stratford' though

in London it was to appear as 'The Merry Wives of Windsor'. So began a long session of translation, with Eleanor transcribing Shakespeare's words in to fluent mouse, until the whole play was complete.

Shakespeare thanked Eleanor for her trouble and promised that the new play would be put on in London, if it proved popular at our mouse theatre in Stratford. She promised to send him news of the plays success. With that Shakespeare had to leave us again and all the mice of Stratford gathered to bid him a fond farewell, as once they had greeted us, when we first arrived with Shakespeare's company of actors long, long ago.

If on a midsummer evening, when the air is warm and thick with dusk, you should stray along the riverbank, till you reach the Dell in the shadow of the church above and there rest still awhile, you might just hear the faintest high-pitched sound. Part the long grass at the foot of the third willow and listen, listen! Is that the faint squeak of a mouse? Is there a greenish glow worm light twinkling through a fragment of stained glass? Lean closer, until your ear touches the cold pane and if you can remember your conversational mouse, you might just hear.

"Kit tell us about the time you went to Windsor and saw Will Shakespeare perform The Merry Wives of Windsor for Queen Elizabeth…"

THE END

By the same author and illustrator:

A Midsummer Mouse

The Memoir of a Theatrical Mouse or 'What you will'

The first book in the series, in which Kit the mouse takes to the stage, fights a pirate and finds true love, all in our own Stratford-upon-Avon. 'A Midsummer Mouse' records Kit's adoption by William Shakespeare's theatre company and their journey to Stratford. Kit becomes an actor and we meet the villainous Black Jack who features prominently in the second book 'The Merry Mice of Stratford'. Further exciting adventures await Kit as the series continues, but that's another story.